D1288460

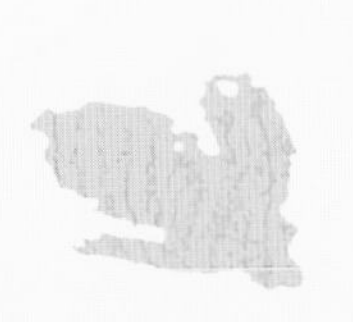

Previously published as *Jhupli's Honey Box* by Tulika Publishers in India in 2022.
First published in English by Amazon Crossing Kids in collaboration with Amazon Crossing in 2023.

Published by Amazon Crossing Kids, New York, in collaboration with Amazon Crossing

www.apub.com

ISBN-13: 9781662514678 (hardcover)
ISBN-13: 9781662514654 (eBook)

The illustrations were rendered in digital media.

Book design by Liz Casal
Printed in China

First Edition
10 9 8 7 6 5 4 3 2 1

JHUPLI'S HONEY BEE BOX

words by
ACHINTYARUP RAY
pictures by
SHIVAM CHOUDHARY

amazon crossing kids

The mango tree stands bowed over the thatched roof. A storm last summer left it a little bent. Jhupli scampers halfway up the tree, swift as a squirrel, and looks toward the river, shading her eyes from the sun. In the river is a motorboat, two fishing boats, and water everywhere. On the other side is dense forest.

She can't see Baba's boat.

It was so very early in the morning when Baba went out. Long before Jhupli woke up. Evening will roll in by the time he gets back. The crows will be back in their nests.

That’s when Baba will walk in past the fence, slightly swaying, holding the heavy tin of honey on his shoulder with both hands. Ma will stop what she’s doing and get up to go help with the tin. Both of them will lower it to the ground—honey dripping down the side, drop by drop.

Jhupli will come and stand close to her father.

Jhupli feels restless now. She worries, runs again to the bank to look for the boat.

Where is Baba?

It will be such a relief once he's back. Then Jhupli will sit with her books, munch some muri.

At night Ma will cook fish, spicy hot. Jhupli and Ma had gone down to the river to catch these tiny fish in the morning. Some of them Ma sold in the market, some were left over. That's what she'll cook into a chochchori. Some nights, Baba gets back really late.

In the morning, Jhupli has to go to school quite early. She and her little brother will go together. From home they will go to the riverbank, and from there by boat. Theirs is the only school in the surrounding islands. So children from other island villages come there too. They study and have lunch—rice, dal, potatoes, and egg curry.

Should I climb up the bank again to look for Baba's boat?
Jhupli wonders. The mudbank is high, and then there's the river.
Their whole island is surrounded by this high mudbank.
If it wasn't there, the whole village would go underwater
when the tide rose and the river swelled.
Why isn't Baba back yet?

Baba once took Jhupli and her brother to school in Haran Kaka's boat. Baba rows a boat so well! But that boat now lies empty by the side of the mudbank. One day, Haran Kaka went into the forest to collect honey and didn't come back.

Jhupli feels sad when she thinks about it. And scared. And worried. For Baba, and for those like him who have to go into the forest. These Sundarban jungles are full of tigers. Those who go in there, go in danger.

Those who go in there might not come back out.

Just as she thinks of this, Jhupli hears footsteps outside.

Baba!

Jhupli and her brother jump down from the house and run to him. Baba smells of sweat, of honey.

Ma brings down the tin from Baba's shoulder. In it is thick golden honey. And broken bits of honeycomb. Baba breaks off a tiny piece and gives it to Jhupli.

Her eyes sparkle in the dim glow of the solar lamp that lights the front of the house.

Happy and relieved, Jhupli clings to Baba.

That night, lying near her father, Jhupli asks,
"Why do you have to go to the jungle, Baba?"

"Because I bring honey from the forest. Others bring wood. We get money by selling all that, and with that money, we buy rice, we buy dal. That's how we have something to cook. What will we eat if I don't go into the jungle?"
Baba's eyes fall closed as he finishes speaking.

Early the next morning, Jhupli gets off the boat to school, grabs her brother's hand, and runs straight to the teacher. She has something on her mind. On the boat, staring out at the jungle, she'd gotten an idea.

"Mastermoshai, can't they make honey at home—my baba and the others? The forest department once gave people honey bee boxes, remember? Shyamu's father got one. It has bees inside, and they make honey. If that honey can be sold at the market, no one needs to go into the jungle. Isn't it true?"

Do you know what Jhupli's teacher did? He thought about it, then he talked to the other teachers. He went from house to house to speak to all the honey-gatherer families, to make them agree. Then he went to the forest department to arrange for honey bee boxes and set them up in every house.

Now, in Jhupli's village, no one has to go into the jungle for honey. No one has to put their lives in danger for food.

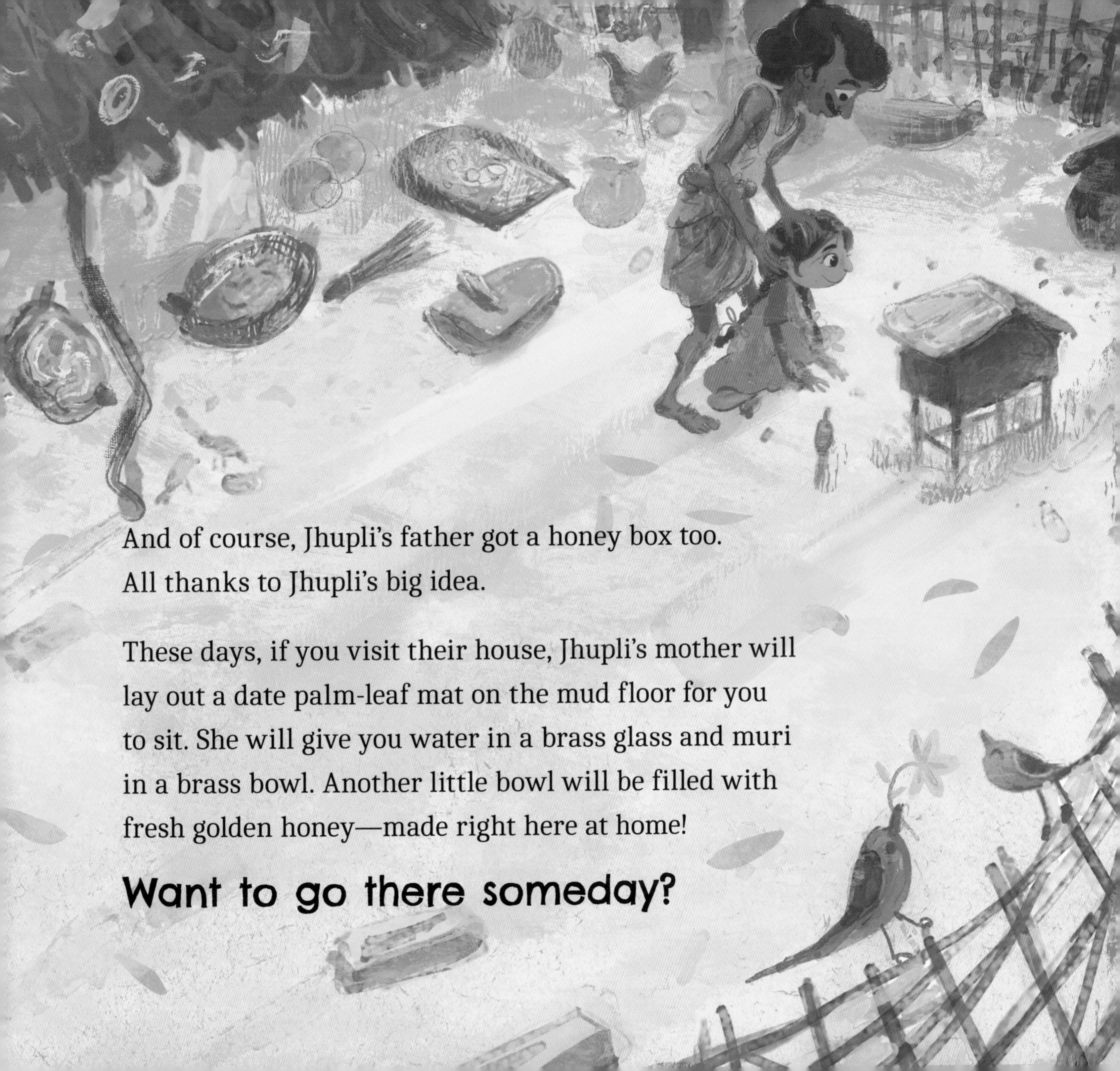

And of course, Jhupli's father got a honey box too. All thanks to Jhupli's big idea.

These days, if you visit their house, Jhupli's mother will lay out a date palm-leaf mat on the mud floor for you to sit. She will give you water in a brass glass and muri in a brass bowl. Another little bowl will be filled with fresh golden honey—made right here at home!

Want to go there someday?

GLOSSARY

baba: Father.

chochchori: A traditional Bengali-style dish of mixed vegetables and/or fish.

dal: A South Asian dish made from lentils or other pulses. Also spelled daal or dahl.

kaka: Uncle.

mastermoshai: A male teacher.

muri: A puffed-rice snack that is popular across India and Bangladesh.

HONEY BEE BOXES

Honey bee boxes are box structures created to house bees and make gathering their honey easy, with the least disruption to the hive. You don't have to be a professional honey gatherer like Jhupli's baba to own and use a honey bee box. In fact, some people even raise bees in their own backyards.

THE HONEY GATHERERS OF THE SUNDARBANS

The Sundarbans is an area stretching across parts of India and Bangladesh that spans a vast river delta, where rivers big and small; their many branches; and many, many small creeks meet with the Bay of Bengal. This region is home to the largest mangrove forests in the world and a huge biodiversity of plants and animals, including the majestic **Bengal Tiger**. The Sundarbans region is also world-famous for its honey. For generations, honey gatherers have risked their lives every spring to harvest this precious honey. They travel in groups, armed with sticks and axes, to protect them from the many dangers of the jungle, including crocodiles, venomous snakes, and most formidably, tigers.